I0598957

Acknowledgements

With heartfelt thanks to Creativa Fay for bringing this story to life through formatting and cover design—your creative touch means the world.

To Sarah Anderson, for your friendship and support as I prepare this tale for its final form.

And to my family and friends—thank you for walking beside me, through storms and stories alike.

Disclaimer

This is a work of fiction. Names, characters, places, and events are either the product of the author's imagination or used fictitiously. Any resemblance to actual persons, living or dead, or actual events is purely coincidental.

The Siren's Cry

Characters

Maria the lighthouse daughter.

Sam the lighthouse Dad

George

The Siren's cry

The sirens called out.

Maria's hair whipped across her face as the cold breeze lashed at her skin. Standing beneath the steady pulse of the lighthouse beacon, she searched the craggy shoreline for her father. The siren's mournful wail echoed again, a sound meant to guide weary sailors to safety. Yet tonight, it carried an ominous weight.

The harbour below was eerily silent, the restless water still save for the gentle sway of the rocky boats that had returned to shore. No sign of life stirred. The cry came again, cutting through the thick darkness, and with a pounding heart, Maria ventured out to find her father.

She knocked at the door of George, the old villager who lived nearest to the cliffs. His wrinkled face creased with worry as she told him of her father's disappearance.

"The sirens only call when a storm's brewing," he muttered, clutching a lantern as if to ward off the shadows. "Best check with your father."

"He's gone," Maria whispered, the fear in her voice undeniable.

Reluctantly, George joined her, and together they hurried into the oppressive black of the night. The siren's wail grew louder, more haunting. And as they neared the shore, Maria's breath hitched. What they thought was just the cry of the sirens seemed to be something more—a cry for help.

By the time they stumbled upon the water's edge, a disturbing truth began to unfold. The sailors hadn't simply vanished. One by one, they had been taken... or so it seemed.

As Maria's tears began to fall, the storm loomed closer, its winds snuffing out what little light remained. The tension in the air was palpable, pressing against her chest. She clung to George's steady presence, their years of familiarity offering the smallest comfort. Her father had trusted George and so had she—for as long as she could remember.

They climbed the path toward the lighthouse, the place she and her father had always called home. Its weathered walls held stories of adventure and nights spent welcoming sailors with tales of the sea. Yet tonight, those walls felt hollow. The light in the tower, so often a beacon of hope, flickered uncertainly, as if echoing her own fears.

"Where is he?" Maria murmured, almost to herself. "And where are the sailors?"

George didn't reply, his eyes scanning the horizon, where the storm churned ever closer to shore. The siren wailed again—a piercing cry lost to the roar of the waves.

Chapter Two: The Brewing Storm

The lighthouse groaned as Maria and George stepped inside, its old bones creaking in the wind. The air smelled of salt and rust, and the walls seemed to hold their breath. George lit the lanterns one by one, their glow soft but steady, chasing shadows into the corners.

Maria ran her fingers along the stone, remembering how her father used to say, "Light doesn't just guide—it listens." Tonight, it felt deaf.

Outside, the wind slowed. The sea lay still, too still.

"Maybe the storm's passed," George said, though his voice didn't sound convinced.

Maria shook her head. "The sirens don't cry for nothing."

They stayed in the lighthouse as night fell, wrapped in silence and worry. Maria couldn't sleep. Her thoughts spun like the beacon above— round and round, always landing on her father. George paced, muttering old sailor sayings under his breath. None of them helped.

The hours dragged. The sea remained quiet, but the air felt heavy, like something was waiting.

Just before dawn, the sirens wailed again—longer, louder, and more desperate.

Maria's heart thudded. "They're calling again," she whispered. "But not for the storm."

George's lantern flickered. "Then what?" he asked, but Maria was already heading for the door.

The sky cracked open. Rain fell like stones, hard and fast.

Waves slammed against the rocks, foaming and wild, as if the sea itself was angry.

Maria shouted her father's name, but the wind swallowed her voice.

Boats bobbed like ghosts in the harbour, empty and broken.

She and George pushed forward, soaked and shivering, searching the shore for any sign of life. The sirens cried again, their sound twisting through the storm like a warning—or a lure.

Maria's breath came in gasps. Her father was out there. So were the sailors.

And whatever had taken them… might not be done yet.

Chapter Three: Beneath the Surface

Maria couldn't sleep. The voice had returned— soft, low, calling her name through the wind.

She waited until George dozed in his chair, then slipped out into the storm.

The sea roared louder than before, waves crashing against the rocks like thunder.

She walked toward the shore, heart pounding, calling out:

"Dad? Are you there?"

A wave rose suddenly, taller than the lighthouse itself.

Maria gasped, tried to run—but the sea was faster.

It swept her off her feet, pulling her under.

She didn't drown.

Instead, she drifted through a strange, glowing world beneath the waves.

The water shimmered with light, and the storm above sounded distant, like a memory.

Shapes moved around her—figures with flowing hair and eyes like moonlight.

The sirens.

They circled her slowly, their voices no longer cries but words.

"You came," they said. "You heard us."

Maria looked around. The sailors were here— floating, silent, caught in a trance.

Her father was among them, eyes closed, lips parted as if dreaming.

"Why?" she whispered. "Why did you take them?"

The sirens' voices echoed like wind through caves.

"The sea remembers. A promise was broken. The lighthouse once kept balance. Now it does not."

Maria's breath caught. "What do you want?"

The sirens paused. Then one stepped forward, her voice like rain on stone.

"A memory. One you hold dear. Give it, and they will be free."

Maria hesitated. She thought of her father—of the night he taught her to light the beacon, of the stories he told, of the warmth in his voice.

She nodded.

The sirens touched her forehead. Light bloomed—
and something slipped away.

She couldn't remember what. Only that it had
mattered.

The sirens sang once more. The sailors stirred. The
trance broke.

Maria woke on the shore, soaked and shivering.

George knelt beside her, lantern in hand.

"You're back," he said, voice trembling. "You're
back."

Behind him, the sailors stumbled from the waves,
dazed but alive.

Her father was among them. He looked at her, eyes
full of wonder—and something else.

Loss.

Maria tried to speak, but the words felt distant.

She couldn't remember the story he used to tell.

She only knew she had loved it.

The sirens were gone. The sea was quiet.

But the lighthouse light still flickered, uncertain.

And somewhere deep below, the sea remembered.

She turned toward the rocks, where the waves crashed hardest. Something glimmered—just for a moment—in the foam. A shape. A figure?

"Did you see that?" she cried, grabbing George's arm.

But he was staring in the opposite direction, eyes wide.

"Maria," he said slowly, "the lighthouse light… it's gone."

She spun around. The beacon, their only guide in the storm, had vanished.

No light. No sound. Just the sirens, growing louder.

Then, from the sea, a voice rose—not the siren's cry, but something else.

Low. Human. Calling her name.

"Maria…"

She stepped forward, heart pounding.

"Dad?"

The voice came again, closer now.

"Maria…"

But George grabbed her hand, his grip firm.

"That's not your father," he said. "Not anymore."
and whatever had taken them… might n Maria
stood at the edge of the shore, watching the sailors
gather.

But not all had returned.

Five names. Five faces. Missing.

George counted again, his voice quiet. "Some
didn't make it."

Maria's chest tightened. She looked out to the
horizon, where the storm had faded into a pale,
trembling light.

There, in the distance, the sea shimmered
strangely—like it was hiding something.

A shape. A shadow. A sorrow.

The sirens had kept their word. But the sea… the
sea had taken its own. Not to be done yet.

Chapter Four: The Sirens' Mercy

The sailors who returned did not speak. They sat by the fire in George's cottage, staring into the flames as if trying to remember who they were.

Maria watched them, heart heavy. Her father was among them, quiet and distant.

He smiled at her, but something in his eyes was missing.

George brought out an old journal, its pages yellowed and soft.

"Found this in the lighthouse," he said. "Belonged to a keeper before your dad."

Maria read the words aloud:

"Never follow the sirens' call. It is not a guide. It is a gate."

She looked up. "A gate to what?"

George didn't answer.

Later, Maria spoke to one of the sailors—a young man named Ellis.

"I remember the light," he said. "Then the song. It was beautiful. I followed it."

He paused, trembling.

"But it wasn't the sirens who pulled me under. It was something else. Cold. Watching. It had eyes."

Maria's breath caught. The sirens hadn't saved them. They had delivered them.

She returned to the lighthouse, searching for answers.

Her father's old story came back to her: "The sea gives, but it never forgets."

She stood at the top of the tower, staring out at the horizon.

The sea was calm now, but the air felt wrong.

Then she heard it—faint, distant, curling through the wind.

The sirens were calling again.

Maria gripped the railing.

She knew now: the call was not a warning. It was a claim.

Chapter Five: The Deepest Truth

The sea was quiet, but Maria knew better.

She stood at the lighthouse with George, the wind tugging at their coats. The sirens' call had faded, but its echo lingered—soft, tempting, dangerous.

"We can't wait," she said. "It'll come again."

George nodded. His face was pale, but his eyes were steady.

"I've lived by this sea my whole life," he said. "But I never truly saw it. Not until now."

They followed the old path down to the cliffs, where the rocks split and the sea whispered secrets. There, hidden behind a curtain of mist, was a cave—dark, deep, and pulsing with unseen energy.

Inside, the air shimmered. The walls glowed faintly, marked with symbols older than the village itself.

Maria felt them hum beneath her skin.

Then the sirens appeared—not the ones she had met before. These were different.

Younger. Wilder. Their eyes held storms.

"You came," they said. "But you are not the first."

George stepped forward. "We want the truth. Why do you call? Why do you take?"

The sirens circled them slowly.

"We do not take. We warn. But the sea… the sea chooses."

Maria's voice was firm. "Then who does the sea serve?"

The cave trembled. A low sound rose from the depths—like a heartbeat, slow and ancient.

"The sea serves memory," the sirens whispered. "And memory is not kind."

Maria understood. The sea remembered every broken promise, every forgotten soul. It called out to balance what had been lost.

George turned to her. "We can't fight the sea. But we can remind it."

He stepped into the center of the cave, raised the lantern high, and spoke:

"We remember the five. We remember the promise. We remember the light."

The cave pulsed. The sirens stilled.

Then, slowly, the symbols on the walls faded. The heartbeat quieted.

Epilogue: The Five

The village never forgot the five.

Their names were carved into the stone wall beside the lighthouse, where the sea could see them. Flowers were placed there each year, and lanterns lit on stormy nights.

Maria often stood before the wall, tracing the names with her fingers.

She couldn't remember the story her father used to tell—but she remembered them.

George kept the journal safe, tucked beneath the floorboards of the lighthouse.

He said it was better that way. Some truths were meant to be remembered quietly.

The sirens never returned in the same way.

But sometimes, on windless nights, a song would drift across the water—soft, sorrowful, and strange.

Maria would listen, hand on the railing, heart steady.

She knew now what the sea wanted.

Not revenge. Not chaos.

Just memory.

And the five… they were part of it, outside the storm began to lift. if she didn't stop it, more would be taken.

DESTINED ENCOUNTER

Characters

Michael: "Michael, impulsive and full of courage, thrived on leaps of faith even when the path ahead seemed shrouded in mystery."

Michelle: "Michelle, cautious and analytical, carried the weight of her thoughts in the gentle adjustment of her glasses and the pages of her journal."

Vera: "Vera, the wise old lady, guarded secrets of the past with a knowing smile and a quiet determination to guide them."

Their friend: "Their friend, fragile but fighting, was the silent reminder of what was at stake and the urgency driving them forward."

The Curse: "The curse, a spectral figure born of bitterness and vengeance, loomed like a dark shadow over their destinies, feeding on fear and fractured bonds."

DESTINED ENCOUNTER

Michelle's glasses were steamed up from her coffee cup, which she had carelessly placed too close to her face. The cozy café buzzed with the soft chatter of patrons and the clinking of cups.

Outside, the rain pattered gently against the windows, creating a soothing melody. She peeped over her foggy lenses and, as she wiped them with a quick swipe of her sleeve, she noticed a stranger standing at her table.

He had a nervous smile playing on his lips, tall with tousled hair, and eyes that seemed to hold a thousand stories. His fingers twitched slightly, turning something small and shiny between them.

"Excuse me," he said, his voice slightly trembling, "I know this might sound strange, but I believe you're my soulmate."

Michelle blinked in surprise, struggling to process the bizarre situation. "How—what—why would you say that?" she stammered. "Why me, and what does it even mean?"

The stranger took a deep breath, his eyes locking into hers with a mix of determination and vulnerability. "It's a long story," he began, "but I promise there's a reason behind all of this."

He reached into his pocket and pulled out an old, tattered photograph. Her eyes widened as she saw herself as a child, standing next to a boy who looked strikingly similar to the man before her.

"This photo," he said, "was taken when we were just kids. We met at a summer camp, and you gave me a locket as a token of our friendship. I promised to find you again, no matter what."

Michelle felt a rush of memories flood back—the locket, the campfire nights, and a promise made under the stars. She remembered the way the campfire crackled, the smell of toasted marshmallows, and the warmth of the friendship they had shared.

"But how is this possible?" she whispered, her voice trembling. "That was so long ago..."

"There's more," he said, his voice dropping to a conspiratorial whisper. "I'm not from this time. I travelled back to this moment because there's something important, we need to do together. Our future depends on it."

Michelle, her mind racing, couldn't help but ask, "What is it we need to do? What is the secret you're hiding?"

The man—Michael, he called himself—glanced around nervously before speaking again. "There's an event coming up—a pivotal moment that will change everything. We have to stop it from happening. In our past, we missed the signs, and it led to disaster."

"But why us? Why are we soulmates?" Michelle pressed, desperate for answers.

"Because," Michael said, his voice steadying with newfound resolve, "our connection spans lifetimes. We've always found each other in different eras, and each time, our bond has been crucial in preventing some catastrophic event. This time is no different. We were chosen because our combined strengths can change the course of history."

He paused, then continued, "The locket you gave me—it holds a secret that can stop a curse. We need to find Vera, the old lady down the road. She was there at the campfire, and she knows our destiny. If we don't lift the curse, our friends will become ill, and worse, the curse will spread."

Michelle nodded, a sense of urgency washing over her. "But what if it's too late for one of our friends?" she asked, her voice trembling with worry.

"We have to try," Michael said firmly. "Vera will guide us. We may need to travel through time to uncover the truth and lift the curse. But no matter what, we must not give up."

Together, they set off to find Vera, knowing that their journey would be fraught with challenges. The streets were eerily quiet as they walked, their footsteps echoing on the pavement. As they knocked on her door, an eerie silence filled the air. The old lady, with her wise eyes and knowing smile, welcomed them inside.

"It's time," Vera said, her voice soft but resolute. "The locket holds the key. You must return to the campfire where it all began and face the curse head-on. Only then can you lift it and save your friends."

With a deep breath, they activated the locket, feeling a rush of wind and light as they were transported back to the campfire. The flames crackled, casting eerie shadows as they faced the spectral figure of the woman who had cursed them.

"You've returned," the figure hissed. "But this time, you won't succeed."

Drawing on their bond and the locket's power, Michael and Michelle confronted the curse. The spectral figure's presence grew stronger, and the air turned cold. They felt a chill run down their spines, but their determination did not waver.

"We won't let you harm anyone else," Michael said, his voice filled with resolve. "We will lift this curse once and for all."

The figure laughed, a sound that sent shivers through them. "You think you can defeat me? The curse is powerful, and your bond is weak."

But they knew better. They focused on their connection, remembering the promise they made under the stars and the strength they drew from each other. The locket glowed brightly, illuminating the dark forest around them.

"Together," Michelle whispered, "we can do this."

As they held the locket between them, its light grew stronger, pushing back the darkness. The spectral figure's laughter turned to a scream as the curse began to unravel. The memories of their past lives, their shared moments of love and friendship, fuelled the locket's power.

The air grew still as the curse lifted, and they felt the weight of the past release its grip. The spectral figure faded into nothingness, and the campfire's warmth returned.

Back in the present, their friend who had fallen ill began to recover, and they knew they had succeeded. As the sun set, they walked hand in hand, their bond stronger than ever.

"Together, we've conquered the past and secured our future," Michelle said, smiling at Michael.

"And we'll face whatever comes next," he replied, "as soulmates, now and always."

Extra passenger

Characters:

Liam: A passenger heading to Spain to meet his girlfriend. He finds himself in the middle of a tense situation on the plane.

Sam: Initially presented as a nervous and suspicious passenger he reveals himself to be a rookie investigator (or air marshal) on his first assignment.

Dan: The enigmatic man at the front of the plane who claims to know more about the situation than he initially lets on. He is later revealed to be an air marshal with inside knowledge.

Captain James: An experienced pilot who is carefully monitoring the aircraft's systems and managing the turbulence with expertise.

Tom: The co-pilot, ready to assist Captain James and take over if needed.

Betty and Minnie: The other two flight attendants working alongside the hostess to manage the passengers and keep them calm. Minnie suggests untying Sam but keeping an eye on him.

Betsy the child: the seven-year-old, travelling with her mum, Carla.

Carla: Betsy's mum with all her secrets.

Sarah: the private detective.

Anna: Dan's girlfriend

John: the know-it-all passenger

The woman and her child about two years old.

<u>Chapter One: The unsettling departure.</u>

Liam nestled into his seat, feeling the exhaustion from the long drive down to Leeds Bradford Airport. He was finally on his way to meet his long-distance girlfriend, Anna, in Majorca, Spain. Anna was a brilliant, thoughtful woman, and he admired her for her intelligence and grace.

This was their first meetup since their school days before she moved away, and Liam's heart raced with a mix of excitement and nervous anticipation.

The air hostess smiled and asked Liam sweetly— or so it seemed. He daydreamed for a moment about what drink to order, but his attention was soon drawn to the next aisle.

There, a weary woman was trying to control her toddler, who looked to be about two years old. By her tired demeanour, it was clear she hadn't had much sleep.

In fact, when Liam turned around, he noticed there weren't many passengers on board. Curiosity got the better of him, and he asked the air hostess how many passengers there were. She smiled and replied, "Only 50 passengers. It's a very rare, quiet flight, likely due to the low season."

As she was speaking, another hostess approached discreetly and whispered something into her ear. The first hostess's expression changed slightly, and she leaned in to inform Liam, "We need to make a brief stop."

Just then, an announcement came over the Tannoy, interrupting the calm atmosphere of the cabin. "Ladies and gentlemen, this is your captain speaking. Due to a minor technical issue, we will be making an unscheduled stop at Airport X. We apologize for the inconvenience and appreciate your understanding."

Liam glanced around, noticing the mixed reactions from other passengers. Some appeared unfazed, while others exchanged curious glances.

As the plane began its descent, a sense of unease settled over him, mingling with his excitement for the upcoming reunion with Anna. Little did he know, this unexpected stop would introduce an unforeseen twist that would change the course of the journey...

As Liam turned away from the other passengers, he couldn't help but notice one of the hostesses looking worried. She seemed to know something, but the chattering and shifting of passengers in their seats drowned out any chance of overhearing.

The atmosphere grew tenser as whispers of concern spread through the cabin. Liam felt a knot of anxiety forming in his stomach, wondering about the unexpected stop.

From a seat in front of him, a frustrated voice broke the murmurs. "This isn't normal, is it? Why do these things always happen when I have a business meeting? After this trip, I'm retiring."

The statement resonated with Liam's own unease, and he couldn't shake the feeling that something unusual was unfolding. The plane continued its descent, and he knew that whatever awaited them at the stopover would bring more than just a minor delay.

As the plane descended after a slight bump, passengers were allowed to stretch their legs before reboarding. However, the boarding process took longer than expected. The passengers were informed that the usual two-hour flight would now take about four hours due to technical issues. This news made the nervous passengers even more anxious.

Liam, wanting some peace on the way back, helped the weary mother with her toddler off the plane. You could see the despair in her face, knowing that if she didn't get back on time, her bully husband would cause her harm. She was thinking about wandering off and getting lost in the crowd to escape her grim reality.

As the passengers milled around the terminal, a new face appeared—a well-dressed man with a confident stride. He slipped into the boarding line, blending in with the crowd. When the call to reboard was announced, the passengers gradually made their way back to their seats, including the new man, who took an unoccupied seat near the back.

The woman with the toddler, feeling overwhelmed, decided not to reboard and disappeared into the terminal. Liam, now back in his seat, glanced around and noticed that the cabin seemed slightly fuller than before. His curiosity piqued, but he dismissed it as an overactive imagination.

Chapter 2: Suspicion and Recognition

As the plane took off again, the captain reassured everyone that the remaining flight would be smooth. Little did they know, the extra passenger on board would soon reveal a hidden agenda that would change the course of their journey... Something was amiss.

John, a know-it-all character sitting a couple of seats away from Liam, caught on too. He leaned towards the air hostess, his voice low but urgent, "Where is the woman with the child?"

"We've already notified the authorities," she replied in hushed tones. John huffed, clearly dissatisfied but let it slide... for now.

When the drinks trolley rolled through the aisle, John's curiosity piqued again. "Who is that person at the back?" he asked, a hint of unease in his voice. "I don't remember seeing him board, but he makes me nervous for some reason."

The hostess nodded, her eyes darting subtly towards the newcomer. "I'll check the passenger records," she said. After a quick glance at her list, she returned, whispering, "He's on the list, but I don't remember him either. Stay vigilant."

Liam's instincts,, from years of training kicked in. He had served in the military for several years, where his keen observation skills had been essential for survival. The new passenger's tense demeanour and avoidance of eye contact didn't sit well with him. The woman's disappearance, combined with the unsettling presence of the new passenger, cast a shadow over the flight. Little did they know, the tension in the air was just the beginning...

Most passengers seemed to relax on the plane, oblivious to anything unusual. They were eating, looking out the window, and falling asleep. As the nervous new passenger began to walk up and down the aisle, his anxiety was evident.

Passengers exchanged worried glances, and whispers of concern spread through the cabin. When he started to act wildly, some passengers decided to restrain him, thinking he was a threat. He called out to stop, but they didn't reassure him until a little girl, aged about 7, went to the toilet and whispered, "It will be okay."

That made him feel at ease, knowing he shouldn't be there—it was mistaken identity, he said in his head.

During the commotion, Liam recognized him. "Sam?" he exclaimed, shocked. Memories of their time in the military together flooded back.

Sam had been a close friend, but their paths had taken different courses. Sam, now pinned down, looked up with pleading eyes.

"Liam, it's me," Sam managed to say. "I... I didn't mean to scare anyone. I've changed, I swear." Liam hesitated, remembering how Sam had always been impulsive, sometimes getting them both into trouble. But this time, there was a genuine fear in Sam's eyes.

"My girlfriend is in Spain too. I'll be joining her after the flight—if we ever get off," Liam said, glancing around the cabin. Quizzical looks from the passengers made him wonder if it was the same girlfriend or a girl with the same name as Sam let it slip. Anna or just a coincidence. Both Liam and Sam were growing increasingly angry.

Sam, his voice trembling, said, "We'll sort this out one way or another when we get off."

Liam's eyes narrowed he was determined. "We will, indeed," he replied.

Chapter 3: Hidden Agendas and Rising Tension

Betsy, the little girl sitting with her mother Carla, felt her heart race. She had hoped to make this journey without any complications, but the rising tension made her secret even harder to keep.

Carla clutched her bag tightly, knowing that what she carried could change everything. Little did she know, her past was about to catch up with her.

Carla lowered her head, trying to avoid Liam's gaze. She couldn't let him see her, not now. Her mind raced back to the stolen money, the life she and her daughter had been fleeing from.

Liam was here, perhaps unknowingly on a collision course with his past. He had been traveling to meet his girlfriend, but there was more to his journey than met the eye.

The real shock lay in the fact that it wasn't Liam who posed the greatest threat—it was Carla. Betsy knew that Liam had been trying to protect her from her own mother's dangerous influence.

The documents in Betsy's bag not her mother's contained proof of the crimes Carla had committed, crimes that Betsy had been trying to expose, but was far too young to understand and had been trying to contact her real dad Liam, but had a panic trying to get his number out of her mums phone without her knowing, but when you're only seven it's not that easy. so, she was shocked to see him on the same flight. But smiled at her dad, from afar but she didn't know all her mums secret she just overheard stuff that she shouldn't,

Betsy glanced at her mother, who was now pretending to be calm, her eyes darting around the cabin, assessing everyone. Betsy knew better.

Carla was more aware than she let on, her mind sharp and manipulative. Betsy had tried to shield herself from the harsh realities of their situation, but there was only so much she could do.

She thought back to the day she discovered the truth about her mother. The documents in her bag were not just evidence of Carla's crimes—they were a lifeline for Betsy. Liam, a former military officer, had stolen the money not for a new life with his school girlfriend, but to ensure Betsy's safety from Carla's reach.

As the plane jolted again, Betsy tightened her grip on her bag. She couldn't afford to let her guard down, not even for a moment. The hostess walked by, giving Betsy a reassuring smile. Betsy forced herself to smile back, but her mind was racing. How much longer could she keep up this charade?

Liam watched them from a distance, his mind racing with plans to protect Betsy. He had to stay vigilant. The court date loomed over them, and the journey to Spain was their last chance to break free.

He just needed to bide his time and wait for the right moment to act. He had to find a way to talk to the marshal, Dan, without raising suspicion.

Dan, seated near the front, seemed engrossed in his own thoughts, occasionally scanning the cabin. Liam knew he had to be careful. Any sudden movement or obvious attempt to communicate could alert Carla. He decided to wait for an opportunity when Carla's attention was diverted.

Betsy, meanwhile, felt the weight of the documents in her bag. The proof she carried was their only chance of exposing Carla's crimes. She glanced at Liam, wondering if he had figured out a way to protect her and ensure their safety.

The stakes had never been higher, and time was running out. She had spoken to her dad in the past and wanted to live with him, but she was worried what her mum would do, her dad had told her in the past when I come back from Spain and at the court, we will sort everything, she felt safe with her dad, but didn't understand all this adult stuff.

As the plane continued its journey, an unsettling calm settled over the cabin. The passengers seemed oblivious to the underlying tension, lost in their own thoughts or sleeping.

But for Liam, Betsy, and Sam, the flight was anything but ordinary. They were each grappling with secrets that could alter the course of their lives.

Betsy knew she had to make a move soon. Her mother's manipulative nature meant that any delay could be disastrous. She waited for a moment when Carla was distracted, then discreetly slid the bag with the documents under her seat and nudged it towards Liam. He noticed and gave her a subtle nod.

Liam took a deep breath, knowing the time to act was drawing near. He glanced towards Dan, hoping the marshal would understand the gravity of the situation. They needed to coordinate their efforts without alerting Carla.

The journey to Spain had become a dangerous game of cat and mouse, with each move carrying significant risks. As the plane neared its destination, the tension reached a breaking point.

Liam, Betsy, and Sam prepared themselves for whatever awaited them on the ground, knowing that their actions in the next few hours could change their lives forever.

As they spoke, the plane jolted again. This time, it wasn't turbulence—it was an in-flight announcement. "Ladies and gentlemen, this is your captain. Due to unforeseen circumstances, we will be making an emergency landing at a nearby airport. Please remain calm and follow the instructions of the flight crew."

Liam's heart raced. He knew this was the moment they had to act.

Chapter 4: The Confrontation:

As the plane continued its descent, the situation grew more chaotic. Both air hostesses, sensing the gravity of the situation, quickly moved through the aisle, checking on the passengers who were showing symptoms. Their calm demeanour contrasted with the growing panic around them.

"Please stay calm, everyone," one of the hostesses urged, though her voice betrayed a hint of worry. "We're going to get through this."

Liam glanced at his watch. Only half an hour until landing. They needed to keep the situation under control. He exchanged a look with Sarah, who nodded and began to assist the hostesses in handing out blankets and water.

The old man's cough had become more persistent, and now others were showing similar symptoms. A woman a few rows back groaned, clutching her stomach, while a young child cried out, "Mommy, I don't feel well."

The passengers who were still healthy started to look around nervously, some pressing their call buttons repeatedly. The atmosphere in the cabin was thick with fear and uncertainty.

Betsy, holding her teddy tightly, whispered to Liam, "What's happening, Dad?"

Liam squeezed her hand, trying to reassure her. "It's going to be okay, sweetheart. We're almost there."

The air hostess made an announcement over the intercom. "Attention, passengers. We have notified the ground crew of the situation. Medical personnel will be waiting for us upon landing. Please remain seated and try to stay calm."

As the plane descended further, Liam's thoughts raced. Could this be another one of Carla's schemes? Or was it something completely unrelated? One thing

Chapter 5: The Final Descent

As the announcement came that they would be making an emergency landing in Spain, the tension in the cabin reached its peak. The flight crew, now working in unison, tried to keep the passengers calm and focused.

Sarah, the private detective, had been observing everything closely. She noticed the unusual behaviour of certain passengers and began to form her own theories about the illness spreading through the cabin. She discreetly approached Dan, the air marshal, and shared her suspicions.

"Dan, I think the illness might be linked to something on board. We need to isolate the source before we land," she whispered urgently.

Dan nodded; his expression serious. "I'll start questioning the passengers. We need to act fast."

Meanwhile, Minnie continued to pull blankets off passengers who were showing symptoms, hoping to find a clue. She noticed a pattern: only those with specific blankets were falling ill.

This discovery led her to the stash of blankets at the back of the plane. She inspected them closely and found traces of an unusual pollen.

"Minnie, look at this," she called out to Sarah, who immediately recognized the pollen from a recent environmental report she had read. "This is pollen from a rare plant that blooms in a specific region. It can cause severe allergic reactions in some people."

"We need to secure these blankets and inform the captain," Sarah said, her voice steady despite the gravity of the situation.

As the plane made its final descent, Dan confronted Carla and the mysterious man at the front, who were now both under suspicion.

Carla's facade crumbled, and she confessed that she had unknowingly brought the contaminated blankets on board as part of a smuggling operation.

Carla's Smuggling Operation

As the plane landed smoothly, medical personnel quickly boarded to assist the ill passengers. Security forces, alerted by Dan, apprehended Carla and the mysterious man as they tried to slip away with the crowd. The passengers, though shaken, were relieved to be on solid ground.

Liam reunited with Betsy, who clung to him tightly. "Dad, I was so scared," she whispered.

"I know, sweetheart. It's over now. We're safe," Liam reassured her, his voice filled with relief.

The passengers were transported to a secure medical facility where they were treated and debriefed. The truth about the contaminated pollen and Carla's smuggling operation slowly emerged, shocking everyone.

Liam, Sarah, and Dan worked together to ensure that the authorities were fully informed, and that Carla's criminal connections were exposed. Betsy, finally free from her mother's influence, looked forward to a new life with her father.

The ordeal had been a harrowing experience, but it also brought to light the strength and resilience of those on board. As they prepared to continue their journey to Majorca, the passengers knew that their lives had been irrevocably changed, but they were determined to move forward with newfound hope and unity.

Chapter 6: New Beginnings

The sun began to rise over Majorca, casting a warm, golden light across the island. The morning air was filled with the scent of blooming flowers and the gentle sound of waves lapping against the shore. It was a new day, full of promise and new beginnings.

Liam stepped out onto the balcony of their hotel room, feeling a sense of peace wash over him. The events of the past few days had been harrowing, but he was grateful to have come through it with Betsy by his side. As he looked out over the ocean, he heard the door behind him open and turned to see Anna.

"Liam," Anna said, her voice filled with relief and joy. She rushed into his arms, and they embraced tightly. "I was so worried about you and Betsy."

"We're here now, safe and sound," Liam reassured her, his voice filled with emotion. "I missed you so much."

Anna smiled, her eyes shining with tears. "I missed you too. Let's make the most of our time together."

Meanwhile, in another part of the hotel, Sam was nervously pacing the lobby, waiting for his own reunion. He glanced at his watch, his heart racing with anticipation. Just then, the elevator doors opened, and Anna stepped out.

"Sam!" she exclaimed, her face lighting up as she saw him.

Sam's heart leaped at the sight of her. He rushed forward and pulled her into a tight hug. "Anna, I can't believe we're finally together."

Anna looked up at him, her eyes filled with love. "I've missed you so much. Let's never be apart again."

As the morning unfolded, the hotel lobby buzzed with the reunions of passengers who had endured the ordeal together. Liam, Betsy, Sam, and the two Annas joined the group, sharing their stories and laughter. The bonds they had forged during the crisis had only grown stronger, and they knew that their lives had been changed forever.

One evening, as they all gathered for a dinner at a charming local restaurant, the two Annas began to share more about their lives in Spain.

"It's funny," said Sam's Anna, "I moved here to be closer to family. My cousin lives in the neighbouring villa."

Liam's Anna nodded, "Really? I have family here too! My cousin recently moved into the neighbouring villa."

They both paused, then laughed as the realization dawned. "Wait, you don't mean...," Sam's Anna started.

Liam's Anna gasped, "Are you saying we're cousins?"

It turned out that both Annas were indeed cousins, and they lived right next to each other in Spain. The group burst into laughter and cheers, amazed at the coincidence and the joy it brought to their newfound friendships.

Liam looked around at the smiling faces of his new friends and felt a sense of gratitude. The journey had been difficult, but it had also brought them closer together. As the sun continued to set, he knew that they were all stepping into a new dawn, filled with hope and endless possibilities.

Summoned the vanished

Characters:

Elisha – Thoughtful, cautious, with a quiet determination. She's more reluctant but deeply perceptive.

Ellie – Bold, quick to act, more rebellious than her counterpart—fearless when facing the unknown.

Annie – The Unyielding Mother The mother who never turned away – The villagers will shun her. They will pretend she is gone. But she knows the truth. She has seen the cracks in their fear. And now, she will follow her children beyond the road no one speaks of—because she knows they are not lost. They are waiting.

Prologue: The Field That Calls

They never meant to meet his eye.

The field had been nothing more than a quiet stretch of land—untouched, unspoken, always there but never truly seen. It beckoned without words, inviting without warning. It felt no different from the paths they had walked since childhood, no reason to fear its silence, no reason to believe they had done anything wrong.

And yet—they had.

The stranger had been waiting.

His gaze found them before they had even realized they were looking. A moment too long, a breath held too tight. His whisper did not reach their ears, yet somehow, it lingered in their mouths—like a word half-spoken, a name they had never known but suddenly understood.

They never meant for it to happen.

But neither had the others.

The ones who had stepped too far before them.

The ones whose names had been swallowed by silence.

The ones who vanished.

And now, standing on the threshold of the forbidden, they wondered—did the others ever intend to leave? Or had something taken them before they could decide?

Because now, the weight of it pressed against them—the truth of every whispered warning, the echo of every footstep that never returned.

And yet, despite the fear, despite the certainty that the boundary was more than just a line in the dirt, they crossed.

Chapter One: The Summons

Elisha and Ellie stood side by side, their matching blue dresses pressed and perfect, though the damp church air made the fabric cling to their skin. Their legs ached from standing so long, but neither dared shift beneath the weight of the villagers' stares.

There were twenty sets of eyes in the room— watchful, unkind. Another five elders absent; their warnings carried in whispers passed from one row to the next. The silence felt thicker than the candle smoke curling toward the rafters.

"Do you have any idea what you've done?"

The pastor's voice cut through the stillness, low and measured. His gaze did not waver.

Elisha opened her mouth, then closed it. The words weren't coming.

The village mothers whispered behind their hands, but none of them dared speak. Even Ellie's and Ellas own mother sat stiff-backed in the second pew, hands clasped so tight that her knuckles had gone white. She had not looked at her daughters once since they were brought in.

"It was just a field," Ellie finally managed, but the second she spoke, someone gasped.

A sharp crack rang out as the pastor's palm slammed onto the pulpit. "Do not speak of it."

A breeze found its way through the church doors, carrying the scent of earth and damp grass—remnants of the place they should not have been. The place beyond the village boundaries. The place where they had seen him.

Elisha swallowed hard, but the lump in her throat remained. The stranger.

She hadn't even thought about it at the time—not in the way the elders wanted her to. She had only seen a man, standing at the edge of the forbidden field. He had looked normal. He had spoken gently, but they did not tell them that.

And yet, here they stood. Summoned. Shamed.

Punished.

"What did he say to you?" the pastor asked.

Elisha and Ellie did not answer.

They could not.

Because the truth was, the stranger had not spoken at all, not really only a passing quiet word for them only to hear,

"He had only smiled", they said.

And the village had known—had felt it, even from the other side of town. Something had changed the moment the girls had locked eyes with him.

<u>Chapter Two: The Crossing</u>

The morning after the summons, the air in the village felt different—thicker, heavier, as if carrying something unspoken.

Elisha and Ellie walked through the narrow streets, their stomachs tight with hunger, their hands empty. No one would sell to them. No one would speak to them. It was as if they had never existed.

Ellie tugged at Elisha's sleeve. "We need food, money… something."

But the villagers turned away whenever they approached, avoiding eye contact, keeping their doors shut. A woman who had once braided Ellie's hair hurried past without a glance.

"They're afraid," Elisha murmured.

"They hate us," Ellie whispered back.

Near the old well, George—the merchant—was stacking sacks of grain. Elisha stepped forward, hoping he'd break the silence, but before she could ask, he kicked dirt over their footprints, as if erasing proof, they'd ever been there.

The message was clear: they wouldn't survive here much longer.

Then—a whisper.

"Take what you can and leave."

Elisha whipped around. No one. Just the wind stirring dry leaves.

Then, something shifted behind the well.

A figure.

The stranger stood half-hidden in shadow, watching them. His expression wasn't urgent like before—it was patient, waiting.

Ellie stepped closer. "What do you want?"

He didn't answer. Instead, he nodded toward the back of the merchant's stall, where coin sacks sat, untouched. A silent offer.

Elisha hesitated. Was this a trick? A test?

A red herring.

Ellie clenched her fists. "We're taking it," she said, already moving.

Elisha knew there was no time to second-guess. No time for guilt. She grabbed what they needed— bread, a flask of water, coins—and ran.

Behind them, the stranger did not follow. He only watched.

And as they fled, the last thing Elisha saw was his faint smile, disappearing into the mist—leading them toward something far beyond the village.

And now, the village would never be the same.

Chapter Three: The Warning

Elisha and Ellie had seen fear before. They had felt it in the hushed voices of the elders, in the way their neighbours looked past them as if they weren't there. But this—this was different.

It wasn't just fear. It was expectation.

Someone had been waiting for them to cross.

As they moved deeper into the field, past the last point of familiarity, the world seemed to change. The air grew heavier, thick with something unspoken. The ground beneath their feet felt less like earth and more like something forgotten.

Then, the sign.

Not a real sign—not written words or carved warnings—but something left behind. A message, half-buried in the overgrown grass.

A scarred locket. A torn scrap of cloth. A name, scratched into the wood of an abandoned post—the name of one of the vanished.

Ellie touched the engraving, running her fingers over the letters as if expecting them to burn. "They were here."

Elisha swallowed hard. "Not just here. Waiting."

Then, the presence returned. The same one they felt in the church, in the whispers, in the places where no one dared look for too long.

A watcher. A guardian. Or something worse.

The silence around them was thick, suffocating. And yet, for the first time, they felt something other than dread.

They felt recognition.

Someone—something—knew them.

And somewhere ahead, the vanishers waited.

Chapter Four: The Road Beyond

The fields ended sooner than Ellie had expected. The tall grass that had concealed them faded into uneven terrain—rock-strewn paths, broken by tangled roots that reached like fingers from the earth.

It felt old. Untraveled.

Or rather travelled once but long abandoned.

The silence wasn't ordinary. It pushed against them, pressed into their skin like something alive. There were no birds, no rustling leaves, only the distant hum of a wind that carried no scent, no warmth—just emptiness.

Then came the first sign.

At the edge of a narrow ridge, a marker stood. Faded, worn, carved into splintering wood. Not a name, not a warning—just a single symbol. Something neither of them recognized.

But it wasn't alone.

Elisha stepped forward, running her fingers over the grooves. Not deep enough to be fresh. Not old enough to be forgotten.

Someone had been here.

Ellie exhaled, staring past the marker toward the next stretch of road. It twisted downward, into the mist—a place where shapes shifted in the distance, where the land blurred between real and imagined.

Then, she saw it.

A figure.

Far ahead, barely visible a watching silhouette, still, unmoving.

It wasn't the stranger from before. It was someone else.

Elisha's pulse quickened. This was not the first time they had been watched.

But this time, the presence did not disappear.

It lingered.

Waiting.

Chapter Five: The Path That Wasn't There

The road beneath them shifted. Not physically—there were no cracks splitting the ground—but something had changed. Every step felt heavier, as if the land itself was testing them.

Ellie ran her fingers over a jagged rock jutting from the earth, its surface smooth on one side, fractured on the other. A reminder that something here had broken once—and had never healed.

"Elisha."

Ellisha turned, but Ellie wasn't looking at her.

She was looking past her.

The stranger stood at the road's bend, unmoving, watching.

He had not followed them. He had been waiting.

And this time, he wasn't alone.

Further back, another figure—a woman.

Elisha's breath caught in her throat. Mum.

Her mother's dress was dusted with dirt, her hair windblown, her fists clenched as if she had fought through the village, through whispers, through silence, all to reach them.

"She found us," Ellie whispered.

But Elisha wasn't certain.

Because behind their mother—no one had followed.

The village did not come looking for them.

She was alone.

Shunned.

Because she had broken the rule just by searching.

The stranger turned, facing Elisha and Ellie fully now. And something in his eyes was different. Not curiosity. Not warning.

Recognition.

He knew who they were.

He knew their mother.

And he knew what was beyond the road.

Chapter six: The Chase Through the Forgotten

Annie froze.

The watcher stood at the edge of the field, barely recognizable beneath the shifting mist—but she knew him. The moment their eyes met, something passed between them. Not fear. Not warning.

Recognition.

Elisha and Ellie saw it too—the way their mother's breath hitched, the way her fists clenched as if holding back something unspoken.

Then, the watcher raised a hand.

Not to stop them. To wave them forward.

Ellie didn't hesitate. She grabbed Elisha's wrist and ran.

The field blurred around them, tall grass whipping against their legs as they scrambled forward. The earth beneath their feet felt wrong, shifting like something unsettled. Annie was close behind, her breath sharp, her steps urgent.

Then—movement behind them.

Not just the watcher. Others.

Figures emerging from the mist, their shapes indistinct, their presence undeniable. They weren't villagers. They weren't strangers.

They were something else.

"Elisha, faster!" Ellie shouted, pulling her sister toward a narrow path that cut through the field—a road off the beaten track, hidden beneath tangled roots and broken stone.

They didn't know where it led.

But they had no choice.

The chase tightened. Footsteps pounded behind them, closing in. The mist thickened, swallowing the edges of the world, turning everything into a blur of movement and breath.

Then—the ground dropped beneath them.

Ellie stumbled first, her foot catching on a jagged rock. She tumbled forward, crashing into Elisha, sending them both sprawling onto the uneven terrain. Annie skidded to a stop beside them, her gaze snapping upward.

Ahead, the field ended.

But beyond it—something new.

A place they had never seen before.

A place no one had spoken of.

The mist parted, revealing structures, half-buried in the earth, worn by time but unmistakably built. Not ruins. Not remnants.

A world beyond the village.

And as they stared, breathless, the figures behind them stopped.

Not because they had given up.

But because they could not follow.

Chapter seven: The World Beyond the Field

Elisha's pulse hammered.

The figures stood at the edge of the field, unmoving, watching—but they did not cross.

They couldn't.

Annie stepped forward, her gaze sweeping over the structures ahead. They weren't like the village. They weren't like anything she had ever seen.

Ellie exhaled sharply. "What is this place?"

Annie didn't answer.

Because she knew.

Not everything. Not the full truth. But enough to understand that this place—this forgotten world—was not abandoned.

It had been hidden.

And now, they had found it.

Elisha turned back toward the watcher, still standing at the boundary. His expression had changed. No longer just recognition.

Expectation.

"You knew we'd come here," Annie murmured.

The watcher nodded.

And behind him, the mist began to shift— revealing something else.

Something waiting.

Chapter eight: The Truth Beneath the Mist

Elisha, Ellie, and Annie stood frozen, staring at the world beyond the field.

It wasn't ruins. It wasn't empty.

It was alive.

Buildings, half-buried in the earth, pulsed with faint light—not abandoned, but waiting. The air shimmered, bending like heat waves, revealing glimpses of people moving through the mist.

The vanished.

They were here.

Ellie took a step forward, but Annie grabbed her wrist. "No. We don't belong here."

Elisha turned back toward the watcher. "What is this place?"

The watcher finally spoke.

"You were never meant to see it."

The ground shook.

Behind them, the figures that had chased them moved closer, their hesitation fading. They had waited long enough.

The hidden world was not meant to be found—and now, it was reacting.

The mist tightened, curling around their ankles, pulling them toward the unknown.

Annie fought back, dragging her daughters toward the edge of the field. "We're leaving."

But the watcher blocked their path.

"You cannot leave unchanged."

Chapter nine: The Escape That Wasn't

The mist rose, swallowing the sky, the ground, everything.

Elisha and Ellie ran, their mother close behind, but the world shifted around them. The field was gone. The village was gone.

Only the watcher remained.

"You crossed the boundary," he said. "You cannot return as you were."

Ellie clenched her fists. "Watch me."

She lunged forward, breaking past him, dragging Elisha with her. Annie followed, pushing against the mist, against the unseen force that tried to hold them back.

Then—a crack in the air.

A tear in the mist.

Through it, they saw home—the village, the church, the well. But something was wrong.

It was empty.

Silent.

As if they had never existed.

Elisha's breath hitched. "What did we do?"

The watcher smiled.

"You were never meant to leave."

Chapter 10 Breaking the Whispers

Elisha, Ellie, and Annie stood at the edge of the village, watching the people move like shadows—silent, unaware, trapped in whispers that had erased them.

They weren't just ignored.

They were forgotten.

Elisha clenched her fists. "We have to fix this."

Ellie turned to their mother. "How do we free them?"

Annie looked back toward the field—the place where the hidden world had bled through. The watcher was gone, but the mist still lingered, curling at the edges of reality.

"The whispers came from the crossing," Annie murmured. "If we break the boundary—if we force the worlds together—maybe we can undo it."

But there was a risk.

The hidden world had been sealed away for a reason.

And if they shattered the barrier, they didn't know what would happen.

Ellie exhaled sharply. "Then we do it."

Chapter 11: The Collision

They returned to the field, standing at the place where the mist had first swallowed them.

Elisha pressed her hand against the air—it rippled, like water disturbed by a stone.

Ellie grabbed a broken branch, lifted it high, and struck the boundary.

The mist shuddered.

The ground cracked.

And then—the explosion.

A roar tore through the air, shaking the earth, splitting the sky. The mist collapsed inward, pulling the village, the field, the hidden world into a single, chaotic moment.

Light erupted, blinding, burning, consuming everything.

Elisha screamed, reaching for Ellie, for Annie, but the force ripped them apart, throwing them into the unknown.

Then—silence.

Chapter 12: What Remains

Elisha woke to ruins.

The village was gone.

The field was gone.

Only rubble and trees remained—twisted, unnatural, growing through the remnants of houses, curling around broken stone.

Ellie stirred beside her, coughing, eyes wide with shock. "Where are we?"

Annie stood, surveying the wreckage. "Not where we were."

Because something had changed.

The villagers—the ones who had been trapped in whispers—were here.

But they weren't the same.

Their eyes held memories of the hidden world. Their voices carried echoes of something ancient.

They had never belonged to the village at all.

They had always been part of the other world.

And now—the worlds had merged.

Elisha turned, searching for the watcher.

But he was gone.

Or maybe—he had never been just one person at all.

Maybe he had been all of them.

Ellie exhaled, staring at the strange new landscape—the trees growing through stone, the mist curling at the edges of reality, the new world they had created.

"What do we do now?"

Annie's gaze was steady.

"We survive."

The Truth About the Stranger

As they turned to leave the wreckage behind, Elisha caught sight of something half-buried in the dirt—a scarred locket, its surface worn, its chain broken.

She knew it.

She had seen it before.

In the field.

In the whispers.

In the name scratched into the wood.

Her breath hitched.

The stranger had never been a stranger at all.

He had been one of the vanished.

And now—he was free.

Final Chapter: The Twist That Changes Everything

Elisha, Ellie, and Annie stood among the ruins, staring at the world they had unknowingly created. The village was gone, the field erased, replaced by something new—a place where the whispers had bled through, where the hidden world had merged with their own.

The villagers who had survived were different. Their eyes held memories of the other side; their voices carried echoes of something ancient.

They had never truly belonged to the village.

They had always been part of the other world.

And now, so were Elisha, Ellie, and Annie.

Then, she saw it.

A figure, standing at the edge of the ruins, barely visible through the mist.

Not the watcher.

A stranger.

But Annie was beside her.

Elisha's breath caught.

The figure smiled, just like the watcher had.

Just like the vanished had.

And as the mist curled around them, as the whispers returned, she realized the truth.

They had never escaped.

They had only become part of it.

The figure smiled, just like the watcher had.

Just like the vanished had.

Just like someone who had never truly left.

And as the mist curled around them, as the whispers returned, she realized the truth.

They didn't free the vanished.

They joined them.

THE END.

The Escape Route

Characters:

Janice (Main Character)

Determined and resourceful, caught in a dangerous chase involving mysterious documents.

Carl (Friend of Janice):

Loyal and quick-thinking friend supports Janice in unravelling the mystery.

Dr. Sasha Smith (Medical Researcher):

Intelligent and trustworthy researcher helps decipher the documents' significance.

Grant (Pursuer 1):

Relentless and calculating operative from a private security firm, determined to retrieve the document.

Swaine (Pursuer 2):

Resourceful and driven partner of Grant, equally determined to complete the mission

Jim: the policeman friend of Sasha.

Ann: the colleague of Jim.

Chapter one: Road to Danger.

Janice sat nervously in the waiting room, clutching a folder of documents to her chest. It wasn't an ordinary office she worked at; it had high-security measures and stringent access controls. She had always known her job held some importance; it led to such dangerous situations.

The events that followed were a whirlwind. It began when she and her friend Carl discovered a set of documents that seemed to hold secrets far beyond their comprehension. It appeared to be medical research, but something about it didn't sit right with them.

"We need to get this to someone who can help us understand it," Janice said, her voice trembling.

Carl nodded, equally anxious. "Let's get moving. The longer we hold onto this, the more danger we're in."

As they hurried out of the building, they noticed two men in dark suits watching them intently. Janice's heart raced. "We need to lose them," she whispered to Carl.

They managed to blend into the crowd, making their way to the train station. The rhythmic clatter of the tracks barely masked the sound of their pounding hearts as they reviewed the documents on the train. Carl squinted at the pages. "This isn't just about cancer. It looks like other research too, but parts of it are missing."

Janice nodded, trying to process the gravity of the situation. "Those men seemed desperate to get it back. We have to stay one step ahead of them."

The tension was noticeable as they devised a plan to escape and figure out what the documents truly contained. Their journey had only just begun, and they had no idea what dangers lay ahead.

Chapter Two: The Missing Pieces

We read over the documents carefully as the train sped along, the rhythmic clatter of the tracks barely heard over the pounding of my heart. My friend Carl squinted at the pages. "I don't think this document is just about cancer. It looks like other stuff, but some of it is missing. Where do you think it is? And those men in the blue car—they seemed desperate to get it back."

I nodded, my mind racing. "We need to get this to someone who can help us decipher it. But first, we have to lose these guys."

The men in dark suits were methodically searching each train car. We ducked into a restroom, far too cramped, trying to think of a plan. "We need to create a diversion," Carl whispered. "Something to throw them off our trail."

We then hid quickly behind the buffet cart cupboard, contorting ourselves into small balls as humanly possible. The smell of stale coffee and old pastries filled our nostrils, but we held our breath, trying to stay as still as possible.

Through a crack in the cupboard, I could see the men moving closer, their eyes scanning every corner. My heart pounded so loudly I feared they might hear it. I clenched my fists, praying they wouldn't check behind the buffet cart. Luckily for us, the buffet attendant was refilling in the buffet room and hadn't seen us. When he came back, he winked, realizing something was up but just let us creep out of there. He was a bit amused, and we said see you on our return journey and he smiled an amused laugh.

Just as they were about to approach our hiding spot, an announcement echoed through the train: "Next stop in five minutes."

The men exchanged quick glances. One of them pulled out a phone and spoke quietly, but I caught a glimpse of his name tag clipped to his belt—Grant. The other man, whose name tag read Swaine, nodded, and they reluctantly turned away, heading back towards the front of the train. I exhaled quietly, feeling a wave of relief. We had a small window of time to make our move.

When we thought the coast was clear, we crawled out from behind the cupboard and made our way to the nearest exit. The train began to slow down as it approached the station. "This is our chance," I whispered to Carl. "Let's go."

We disembarked quickly, blending into the crowd of passengers. Glancing back, we saw Grant and Swaine still on the train, their frustrated expressions barely visible through the windows as the train pulled away.

We hurried through the station, our steps echoing on the concrete floor. We had managed to escape, but the danger was far from over. With the document still in our possession and another part hidden by Carl, we needed to stay one step ahead of our pursuers.

As we made our way through the bustling train station, Carl's demeanour shifted. He seemed more tense and hesitant than before. "Carl, what's wrong?" I asked, noticing his anxious glances.

"There's something I need to tell you, Janice," Carl said, his voice low. "This document... it's a ruse. The cancer cure is real, but there's another part—another document that I've hidden. It contains even more groundbreaking research, but I couldn't reveal it before because it's incredibly dangerous if leaked."

I stared at him, trying to process this new information. "Why didn't you tell me earlier?"

"I didn't want to put you in more danger," Carl replied. "But now that we're in this mess, you need to know. The other document outlines research on an immortality tablet. The tablet can extend human life significantly, but it has strange side effects, and there's a one in ten chance that it could be fatal."

My mind raced as I tried to comprehend the gravity of the situation. "We need to get both documents to Sasha. She'll know what to do."

We made our way to the secure location, constantly checking for any signs of Grant and Swaine. When we finally reached Dr. Sasha Smith's lab, she greeted us with a concerned expression. "What's going on, Janice? You sounded urgent on the phone."

I handed her the document we had and explained everything Carl had just revealed. Sasha's eyes widened as she realized the full extent of the research. "We need to secure both documents immediately. This information is too valuable and dangerous."

Together, we devised a plan to retrieve the hidden document and ensure that both sets of research were protected. Our journey was far from over, but with Sasha's expertise and our determination, we were ready to face whatever challenges lay ahead.

Chapter Three: The Hidden Secret

"How do you even know each other? You're not a medical researcher like Sasha here, are you?" Janice asked, curiosity piqued.

"Well, no, but I'm a clinical trial organizer," Carl replied.

"Oh, I thought you took blood samples. Silly me," Janice said with a chuckle.

"Well, that's how we sort of met, wasn't it?" Carl said.

"I was on a trial because I needed the money, but it wasn't a bad one. It was an easy trial," Janice explained. "It was just a cream for eczema to see the side effects. I lost my job but have a new one now, but I won't have one if I don't go tomorrow."

The next day Grant and Swaine, Janice and Carl made their way back to the train station, hoping to retrieve the second Mini and the remaining documents. They blended into the morning rush, cautiously scanning their surroundings for any sign of Grant and Swaine.

As they boarded the train, Janice whispered, "We need to keep a low profile. They could be anywhere. I had to get to work too."

The train ride was tense, filled with stolen glances and hushed conversations. As they approached their stop, Carl saw a familiar face in the crowd—Grant. "He's here," Carl muttered. "And he's not alone."

Swaine, following closely behind, seemed more determined than ever. They disembarked quickly, weaving through the bustling station and making their way to the parking lot where the Minis were parked.

They found their Mini, but the other Mini—the one with the remaining documents—was missing. Panic set in as they realized their mistake. "We need to find it," Janice said urgently. "We can't let them get the other half."

Just then, Grant and Swaine appeared, blocking their path. "Looking for something?" Grant sneered, holding up the keys to the second Mini.

Janice took a deep breath, trying to keep her cool. "You're making a big mistake, Grant. Those documents are dangerous. We need to get them to the right people."

Grant's expression faltered for a moment, but he quickly regained his composure. "Why should I believe you?"

"Because I was your temporary wife for the college thing, but I didn't recognize you till now. You changed your look—well, more mature," Janice said, giggling a bit as Carl gave her strange looks. "I will explain later, it's back in the day," she added, her voice steady. "And I know you're not a bad person. You're just caught up in something bigger than you realize."

Grant hesitated, the weight of her words sinking in. Swaine, however, was not sure what to do.

In the chaos that followed, Janice and Carl managed to slip away, grabbing the documents from the second Mini. It must have been arranged through Grant to be at the train station, Janice thought, and exactly the same blue car as hers. Realizing the easy mix-up—just one year's number plate difference—she thought Carl must have known. Diving into their own car, he admitted to her, "Sorry, yes, I'm caught up in it, but not the big picture. I just needed money.

Chapter Four: The Revelation

Janice and Carl drove in silence, the weight of their predicament hanging heavy in the air. As they navigated through the city streets, Janice's mind raced with the implications of Carl's confession and the dangerous game they were now playing.

"Why didn't you tell me sooner?" Janice finally broke the silence, her voice tinged with frustration and betrayal.

Carl sighed; his eyes fixed on the road ahead. "I was trying to protect you. I didn't want to drag you into this mess any more than you already were."

Janice shook her head, her emotions a mix of anger and confusion. "Protect me? You should have trusted me. We're in this together, whether you like it or not."

Carl glanced at her; guilt etched on his face. "You're right. I'm sorry. I should have been honest with you from the start."

As they approached their destination—a secluded safe house on the outskirts of the city—Janice's phone buzzed with a message from Sasha. "I've secured the first document. We need to talk. Come to the lab as soon as you can."

They parked the car and made their way inside the safe house. Janice's mind continued to reel from the revelations. "What exactly is this immortality tablet? Why is it so important?" she asked, her curiosity getting the better of her.

Carl took a deep breath, sitting down at the kitchen table. "It's ground breaking research, Janice. If perfected, it could extend human life significantly. But the risks are enormous. One in ten people who take it could die from the side effects."

Janice's eyes widened in disbelief. "Why would anyone want to risk that?"

"Because the potential benefits are immense," Carl replied. "Imagine the power and wealth that could come from controlling such a discovery. But it's not just about the tablet itself—it's about who controls it and how it's used."

The gravity of the situation sank in as Janice realized the full extent of the danger they were in. "We need to find a way to make sure this research doesn't fall into the wrong hands."

As they sat in the safe house, formulating their next steps, a sudden noise outside caught their attention. Carl peeked through the blinds, his heart racing. "It's Grant and Swaine. They must have followed us."

Janice's pulse quickened. "We need to get out of here. Now."

They grabbed the documents and made their way to the back door, slipping out into the night. The cold air bit at their skin as they navigated through the dark alleyways, trying to stay one step ahead of their pursuers.

As they ran, Janice's mind raced with thoughts of betrayal and survival. She couldn't shake the feeling that there was more to this than Carl was letting on. She knew she had to stay vigilant and trust her instincts if they were going to make it out of this alive.

Chapter Five: The Return to the Office

Janice's heart pounded as she and Carl made their way back to the office under the cover of early morning darkness. The high-security measures that once seemed difficult now felt like impossible obstacles. The building loomed ahead, an imposing reminder of the dangerous secrets it concealed.

"We need to be careful," Carl whispered, his eyes scanning the area for any signs of movement. "Grant and Swaine agreed to meet us here. We can't trust them entirely, but we need their help."

Janice nodded, her mind racing with thoughts of the documents and the truth they held. As they approached the entrance cautiously, Grant used his access card to bypass the main security system. The tension was palpable as they entered the darkened corridors, every creak and shadow heightening their anxiety.

Disabling the Cameras

Grant led them to a small security room near the entrance. "Wait here," he whispered. He and

Swaine slipped inside, leaving Janice and Carl on high alert. Moments later, the security monitors flickered and then went dark.

"We've disabled the cameras temporarily," Grant said, rejoining them. "But we need to move quickly. We only have a small window before the system resets."

Navigating the high security hallways, they finally reached a concealed door. Grant's card worked again, revealing a hidden room filled with confidential files and research data. Janice's pulse quickened as she sifted through the documents, finding pieces of the immortality tablet research and Sasha's name on several pages.

"We need to get these to Sasha," she whispered, the urgency in her voice unmistakable. "This is bigger than we thought."

Just as they were about to leave, the office's alarm system blared, shattering the tense silence. Panic surged through Janice as a night watchman appeared at the doorway, a stern expression on his face.

"Thought you could sneak around, did you?" he taunted. "You're not going anywhere."

The room erupted into chaos. Grant and Swaine, caught off guard, scrambled to react. Janice and Carl, clutching the documents, ducked past the watchman and bolted down the hallway. The blaring alarm echoed in their ears as they raced through the building, the watchman and security team hot on their heels.

Barely managing to evade capture, they burst out of the building and into the cold morning air. Janice's lungs burned, but she didn't dare slow down. They had to get to Sasha's lab. Time was running out, and the truth they carried was more important than evidence.

Chapter Six: The Long Process

Janice, Carl, Grant, and Swaine arrived at Sasha's lab, their hearts still racing from the narrow escape. Sasha immediately got to work, her hands moving with precision and determination as she began rewriting the formula for the immortality tablet.

"This is going to take time," she said, not looking up from her work. "The formula is complex, and eliminating the deadly side effects won't happen overnight."

While Sasha worked on the formula, Janice, Carl, Grant, and Swaine turned their attention to finding the people of the blue Mini who had the original documents

Just as they began to feel a glimmer of hope, the lab's power suddenly went out. Darkness enveloped them, and the hum of equipment fell silent. Panic set in as they realized the sabotage was far from over.

"We're still being watched," Carl whispered, his voice barely audible in the eerie silence.

Sasha managed to restore the power and continued her work with renewed urgency. Hours passed, and finally, she had the new formula ready. They tested it carefully, hoping for the best.

Chapter Seven: Finding the Blue Mini Owners

The Investigation

Before they could proceed, they knew they had to find the owners of the blue Mini who had the original documents. These documents held the key to understanding the full stakes and building trust. Janice, Carl, Grant, and Swaine began their investigation, following leads and clues to track down the owners.

Near Capture

Their investigation led them to a remote location where the blue Mini was last seen. Just as they were about to retrieve the documents, they were nearly caught by the organization's enforcers. A tense chase ensued, but they managed to escape with the documents in hand.

The Revelation

Back at Sasha's lab, they carefully reviewed the documents. The information they uncovered was shocking—the stakes were higher than they had ever imagined. The documents revealed the full extent of the organization's unethical practices and the potential dangers of the immortality tablet.

Chapter Eight: The Revelation

Unethical Testing on Prisoners

With the new information in hand, they decided to proceed with caution. The organization, in its desperation to perfect the tablet, began testing on prisoners. They offered reduced sentences and better living conditions in exchange for participation. This time, the outcomes were more positive, with fewer severe side effects and more enhanced abilities.

Chapter Nine: New Friendships and the Build-Up

Developing Friendships

As the trials continued, Sasha and Carl developed a close friendship. Carl found redemption in contributing positively to the research, and Sasha valued his insights and dedication. Janice, Grant, and Swaine also strengthened their bonds, learning to trust and rely on each other. Despite their rocky start, they became a cohesive team.

The Plan

With the positive results from the prisoner trials, they realized they had a chance to use this research for good. They devised a plan to expose the organization and its unethical practices while highlighting the potential benefits of the tablet if used responsibly.

"We have the evidence we need," Janice said, determination in her eyes. "It's time to take a stand

and make sure this research is used for the right reasons."

Chapter Ten: The Climax

Confrontation

Janice, Carl, Sasha, Grant, and Swaine gather all
the evidence they've collected and devise a plan to
broadcast the truth about the organization's
unethical practices and the immortality tablet to
the world. They decide to use a secure, encrypted
live stream that can reach a global audience.

Broadcasting the Truth

They infiltrate a media station with the help of a
sympathetic journalist who believes in their cause.
The journalist sets up the live stream, and they
begin broadcasting the evidence, including footage
of the unethical testing, the documents they
retrieved, and testimonials from the victims.

"We're going live in 3... 2... 1..." the journalist
says, hitting the broadcast button.

Janice steps up to the camera, her voice steady but
filled with emotion. "To everyone watching, we
have uncovered a dangerous conspiracy. The
immortality tablet you've heard about is not what it
seems. The organization behind it has conducted
unethical testing on vulnerable individuals, causing

severe and fatal side effects. We have the evidence to prove it."

Global Reaction

National Implications

The country where the organization operates initially wants to control the immortality tablet for its own use. They see the potential for power and wealth, but public outrage forces the government to take action. The leaders of the organization are arrested, and the research is seized.

International Reaction

Other countries watch the live stream and have mixed reactions. Some see the potential benefits of the immortality tablet if used ethically, while others are horrified by the unethical practices and the potential dangers. This leads to a global debate on the ethics of such research and the need for strict regulations.

Chapter Eleven: The Resolution

Happy Ending

The organization's leaders are arrested, and the dangerous research is destroyed. Sasha's lab continues to work on ethical scientific advancements. Janice and Carl reflect on their journey, forging a stronger bond and gaining new perspectives on life and trust. New friendships are formed, and they all look forward to a brighter future.

Thank you for respecting the magic and mystery within these pages.

www.ingramcontent.com/pod-product-compliance
Lightning Source LLC
Chambersburg PA
CBHW052007220626
47052CB00004B/1127